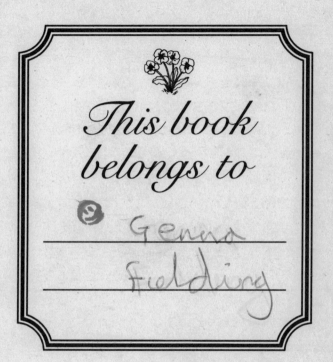

This book belongs to

Genna
Fielding

Genna

The
Smiling
Star

AND OTHER BEDTIME STORIES

The Smiling Star

AND OTHER BEDTIME STORIES

PARRAGON

First published in Great Britain in 1998 by
Parragon
13 Whiteladies Road
Clifton
Bristol BS8 1PB

ISBN 0 75252-534-4

Printed in Great Britain

Produced by Nicola Baxter
PO Box 71
Diss Norfolk IP22 2DT

Stories by Nicola Baxter
Designed by Amanda Hawkes
Text illustrations by Duncan Gutteridge
Cover illustration by Alisa Tingley

Contents

The
Smiling
Star

Every night, when Jenny was tucked up in bed, her mother said the same thing:

"Sweet dreams, darling. Shall we sing our bedtime song?"

And Jenny and her mummy would sing, ever so softly:

> *Star light, star bright,*
> *First star I see tonight,*
> *I wish I may, I wish I might,*
> *Have the wish I wish tonight.*

Then Jenny's mother would give her a kiss and put out the light. With the words of the song still ringing in her head, Jenny would crawl down to the foot of her bed and peep through the curtains. Sometimes it was cloudy, and there were no stars to be seen. In the summertime, it was often too light to see the stars. But when she looked out and saw a dark, clear sky, with little twinkling lights so high up and so far away, Jenny breathed a sigh of happiness. Then she shut her eyes and wished for the thing she wanted more than anything else in the world.

When she was a very tiny girl, Jenny wished for toys, or a visit to the playground, or even something really nice to eat for her supper next day. Sometimes her wishes came true, and sometimes they didn't, but that wasn't really important because they were only little wishes. Now Jenny had a really big wish, and it mattered very much indeed whether it came true or not.

It had all started a few months before. Jenny's mummy and daddy started to have really big arguments. Jenny sometimes found her mummy in tears, although she brushed them quickly away when she saw her little girl. Daddy seemed unhappy too. He hugged Jenny and played with her as much as ever, but at breakfast and supper time, both he and Mummy were unusually quiet, with their eyes on their plates.

Jenny knew that something was badly wrong, and at first she thought it was somehow her fault. She tried to be extra good and helpful. She tried not to talk more than she had to, and she just crept away when the horrid arguments started.

But one day, Jenny's mummy noticed how quiet and good she was being, and asked her what was the matter! Jenny explained that she was trying to make everything all right again, so that they could be a happy family.

Jenny's mummy hugged the little girl and sat her on her lap. She explained very gently that sometimes mummies and daddies don't get along so very well together. She reassured Jenny that it wasn't her fault in any way at all, and she promised that Jenny would not hear any more arguments.

After that, things were a little better. Jenny's mummy and daddy didn't argue in front of her, but Jenny was pretty sure that they still did it in private, because both of them had sad faces and were very quiet when they were together.

Then, one day, Jenny's daddy took her to the park to feed the ducks. As he and Jenny sat together on a bench, he explained that there were going to be some changes.

"I'm going to live in another house in future," he said. "And you and Mummy will move to a little house somewhere very nice. I'll see you ever so often, and we'll have lots of fun together. I love you lots and lots and lots. Everything will be fine."

But Jenny couldn't help bursting into tears.

"I don't want you to go," she sobbed. "Please stay with us."

Jenny's daddy held her close and stroked her hair.

"I have to go, honey," he said. "Mummy and I both think it's the right thing to do, and in the end, we'll all be much happier. You and Mummy will have lovely times together, and when I come to see you, *we'll* have lovely times, too."

Jenny was still very upset, but she tried to be brave. Next day, Daddy didn't come home from work at his usual time.

"Daddy has gone to live in his new house," said Mummy. "And I have found us a lovely little cottage in the countryside. I

know that you will like it, Jenny.
There are cows and sheep and
horses in the fields all around.
And you will be able to have a
rabbit of your own, if you like,
just as you have always wanted."

That night, Jenny and her
mummy sang their special song
as usual:

Star light, star bright,
First star I see tonight,
I wish I may, I wish I might,
Have the wish I wish tonight.

For the first time, after her
mother had closed the door,
Jenny scuttled down to the end

of the bed and peered at the sky as if her life depended on it. Thank goodness! There was one little star, twinkling in the sky.

"I wish my daddy would come home again," whispered Jenny, squeezing her eyes shut. "I wish it with all my heart."

All that week, Jenny made the same wish. Then, on Saturday, some men came with a truck and loaded all the furniture from the house into it.

"Come on, darling," said Jenny's mummy. "We're going to move into our new house today. I know that you will love it. Have you got all your toys?"

Jenny clutched her favourite teddy bear and followed mummy to the car. She looked back at the house where she had been so happy, and tears rolled down her little cheeks.

"It will be all right, honey," said her mummy, hugging her. "I promise it will. New things are often upsetting, but everything will be fine."

"Everyone keeps saying that," sobbed Jenny, "but it isn't fine. It isn't all right."

Mummy started the car and looked as if she might cry too.

"It will be," she said. "Much sooner than you think, it will be."

On the way to the new house, Jenny and Mummy stopped for a snack at a little restaurant. Jenny knew that this was a special treat, and usually she would have loved it. But today the ice cream tasted horrible, and she couldn't finish her milkshake.

"I don't feel very well," she said, pushing her food away.

Mummy felt her forehead and looked at her carefully.

"Then we must hurry up to reach our new home," she said. "You can settle down and rest until you feel better. It's not much farther, and there's a surprise waiting for you there."

The countryside certainly was pretty, as they drove along the winding road to the little village where their new house was to be found. Even Jenny could not help noticing the pretty little lambs jumping in one field. There was nothing like that in the suburbs where she had lived before.

At last Mummy stopped the car and pointed to a little pink cottage with a thatched roof.

"That's where we're going to live," she said. "Isn't it nice?"

Jenny had to agree that the cottage did look pretty. It was the kind of place she had always wanted to live, only she had wanted to live there with her mummy *and* her daddy.

Mummy showed Jenny all over the cottage, including the little bedroom under the eaves that the little girl would have for her very own. Jenny peered out of the window and noticed that there would be a very good view of the stars in the night sky. So *that* would be all right.

"I'm not going to stop wishing just because we've moved here," she said to herself.

"Now," said Mummy, "come outside, and I'll show you your special surprise. Shut your eyes and take my hand."

Jenny followed her mother out into the garden. She felt the sun on her face and could smell lovely scents from the flowers as she passed them.

"Now," said Mummy, "open your eyes!"

Jenny opened them and blinked in the bright sunshine. Then she looked down at a little piece of grass with a fence around it.

"Oh!" cried Jenny. "Is he really for me?"

"Yes," smiled Mummy, for the first time that day. "He's all yours. What are you going to call him, darling?"

Jenny looked at the dear little white rabbit sitting on the grass.

"I'm going to call him Snuffles," she said, "because of the way he's wiggling his nose. Oh, he's

just what I always wanted. Look at his lovely ears and his little pink nose! I'm going to take ever such good care of him."

"I know you will, sweetheart," said Mummy. "I've bought you a little book about how to do it."

"Yes," said Jenny. "I want him to stay with me always. I don't want *him* to go away."

Jenny's mummy said nothing, as she went back into the cottage to start unpacking.

That night, Jenny slept for the first time in her new bedroom. She had her old bed, of course, and all her familiar things about her, but still it felt strange.

Mummy came in as usual to say goodnight and sing the Starlight Song. Jenny could hardly wait for her to close the door. Creeping out of her bed, she went over to the little window and looked out.

How much bigger and nearer the stars seemed than in the town, where the streetlights were

so bright! Jenny gasped as she looked up at the velvety night sky. There was the moon, and there were hundreds and hundreds of little stars twinkling in the darkness.

Jenny looked at one star in particular and made her wish. I'm sure you can easily guess what it was. The star seemed to twinkle as if it was answering her.

Then Jenny crept back into her bed and closed her eyes. It had been a long, tiring day after all.

Almost at once, the little girl heard a tapping on the window. *Tap tap! Tap tap!* it went. Jenny didn't feel at all frightened. She just wondered very much what the strange sound was.

There was nothing else to do. The little girl got out of her bed once more and went to the window. There had not yet been time to put up new curtains, so she could see at once what was making the tapping sound, and she couldn't have been more surprised if Father Christmas himself had been sitting on the windowsill outside.

It was a star! Yes, a shiny yellow star with little arms and legs and a big beaming smile. Jenny rubbed her eyes. She knew that stars didn't come knocking on people's windows in the middle of the night.

But the little star knocked again. *Tap tap! Tap tap!* Almost without thinking, Jenny lifted the catch and opened the window.

"Good evening," said the star. "You wished?"

"Sorry?" said Jenny.

"*I'm* sorry," said the star. "Didn't that make sense? You

wished, so I came. How can I help you this fine starry night?"

"I'm afraid I don't understand," said Jenny. "I've wished lots and lots of times, but I've never seen a star before."

"It's the interference," said the star. "It's a terrible problem for us. In towns there is so much light that children's messages often don't get through. But your wish was beautifully clear tonight. You'd like your daddy to come home, I believe. Now, you will get cold if you keep the window open like this. I'll just hop inside and then we can talk properly. How would that be?"

Jenny was all too happy to invite the star into her bedroom. She hopped back into bed, and the star sat comfortably on the bedside table with his legs crossed. He was still smiling.

"Now," he said, "what has happened to your daddy?"

Then Jenny explained all about the arguments and the new houses. She even told the star about Snuffles.

"I see," said the star. "Poor you. Will you be able to see your daddy sometimes? Or has he gone to live a long way away?"

"Oh no," said Jenny. "He's very near, and he's coming to see me every weekend."

"Well, that is very good," said the star. "Now this kind of thing happens quite a lot, you know, and the best thing to do is always to wait a little while and see how things go. What I would like you to do is to spend a few weeks getting used to your new home. You can have fun with your daddy and with your mummy, and I will come to see you every night to make sure you are all right. Then we will have another little talk and see how things are going."

The star did sound as if he knew what he was talking about,

so Jenny agreed to do just what
he suggested.

The next few weeks passed
more quickly than she could
have imagined. She met lots of
new friends at her playgroup,
and she explored the garden and
the countryside beyond. There
was a nice man who kept bees in
the next cottage, and he had a
little girl too, so Jenny and her

new neighbour often played together.

At the weekends, Daddy came to see Jenny. They had lots of fun and talked about all kinds of things. In fact, they seemed to have a nicer time than they ever had before. Daddy had so often been busy with work from the office or doing jobs around the house at the weekends.

Mummy seemed to be enjoying putting the new house in order too. She made pretty curtains for the windows and a beautiful rabbit hutch for Snuffles, who was as cosy as could be with his straw and his food and water..

All this time, Jenny carried on making the same wish each night. She didn't even have to think about it any more. The words came into her mind as soon as she looked out of her window and saw the stars.

"I wish my daddy could come and live with us," she said.

Each night, the smiling star came to visit Jenny. Sometimes he didn't stay very long, but at other times they sat and talked long into the night. When they had finished, Jenny would open the window, and the little star would whizz right up into the night sky.

The star talked about all kinds of things. He told Jenny about the North Pole and how cold it was there. He explained that it was cold like that in space, too, but that stars didn't mind. He described the many countries that he had seen on his travels and talked about the planets as if they were old friends. He told Jenny about some of the other children he visited, too.

Then one night, he said, "It's time we talked about your first wish, Jenny. I have some questions to ask you."

"All right," said the little girl. "What are they?"

"Would you say that your mummy is happier now?" asked the smiling star.

Jenny thought about hearing her mummy singing as she made Snuffles' rabbit hutch. She remembered the fun they had had together, choosing new things for the house and deciding what to do in the big, rambling garden.

"Yes," she said. "I think she is much happier now."

"And is your daddy happier?" asked the smiling star.

Jenny thought about the way that daddy didn't have those creases in his forehead any more. She thought about all the lovely times she had had with him each weekend. He looked sort of younger somehow.

"Yes," said the little girl. "I think he *is* happier."

"And now for the really important question," said the star. "Are *you* happier, Jenny?"

Jenny thought hard. There were no more arguments. At mealtimes now, she chattered merrily. There were no more awkward silences. And it was lovely living in the country. And then there was Snuffles. She felt so grown up looking after him all by herself.

"Yes," she said. "I do feel happier too."

The smiling star smiled even more broadly. "Then do you think you should make a different wish each night?" he asked. "Why don't you think about it?"

Jenny was rather quiet the next day.

"Are you all right, darling?" asked her mother.

"Yes, I am all right," said Jenny, almost as if she was surprised to find that she was. "We're both all right, aren't we?"

"Yes, we are," smiled Mummy, giving her a hug.

That weekend Jenny asked Daddy if he was all right.

"I'm very all right," laughed Daddy. "Race you to the swings!"

When Mummy came to say goodnight that evening, she sang the special song with Jenny.

Star light, star bright,
First star I see tonight,
I wish I may, I wish I might,
Have the wish I wish tonight.

And Jenny looked out of the window and made a new wish.

"I wish we can all be happy, wherever we live," she said. And you know, her wish came true.

The
Ship of
Dreams

Once there was a mighty ship, with sails of silver and ropes, which are called sheets on a ship, of gold. It had a poop deck and a quarter deck and all the other decks a ship should have. It had portholes and a rudder and masts. But the strange thing is that it didn't have a crew. No, the ship sailed all by itself.

Which ocean did this ship sail upon? Did it cross the great Pacific Ocean or drift across the warm waters of the Indian Ocean? Or did it brave the great storms of the Southern Ocean? No, it sailed none of these great

seas. It sailed the skies. For it was a ship of dreams.

If you go sailing on the ship of dreams, you will visit strange lands and meet people who look almost familiar. You might zoom through the skies or plunge to the bottom of the seas. You could ride on the back of a tiger or take tea with a flea. The ship of dreams can sail anywhere, but it always comes back to port in the morning.

Once there was a little boy who wanted more than anything else to go sailing on the ship of dreams. But in the morning, he could never remember if he had dreamed or not. At school, his friends would talk about the wonderful dreams they had had, but poor Peter could never remember a single one. After a while, he felt so left out that I'm afraid he began to invent dreams that he had not had at all.

"Last night," he would boast, "I dreamed I was riding on a camel. It had a bridle of gold and reins of silver. We travelled over the desert for miles and miles, until we came to a beautiful palace. Everyone bowed down when I went into it. I was the Prince of the whole country, and I owned the palace and everything in it."

"Wow!" said the other children. "I wish we had dreams like that."

"Oh, that was nothing," said Peter. "The night before that I dreamed I was diving in the ocean and saw a wreck on the sea bed. I swam down to it and found a casket full of jewels. They glinted and glittered in the blue water. But just as I was

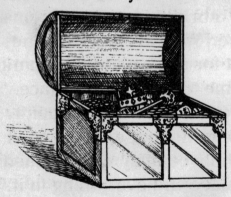

swimming down to reach them, a huge shark came charging towards me. It opened its mouth and…"

"Yes, yes?" cried the children.

"…and I woke up," said Peter.

Peter soon found that everyone wanted to hear about his fabulous dreams. He began to make them more and more elaborate and extraordinary. One day, as he was telling the children about a trip through a forest, where wolves were howling, his teacher happened to overhear him.

"With an imagination like that, Peter," she said, "you should be a writer. You have kept your friends spellbound for an hour."

And when Peter grew up, he did become a writer, a very famous writer. His stories were read and loved the world over.

When Peter was an old, old man, a journalist came to see him to write a story about his life.

"How lucky you were to have such rich dreams to draw on in your early years," he said.

"No," said Peter. "In fact, I did not have dreams at all, but that was lucky too, in a way. I had to use my imagination to make up strange tales for myself, because as far as I know, I never dreamed."

"But everyone dreams!" the young man protested. "It must just be that you don't remember."

"I don't know," said Peter. "I only know that as far as I'm concerned, the ship of dreams has never stopped for me, and I would give all the stories I have ever written and all the money I have ever made for one trip upon that wonderful ship."

The journalist left the old man sitting looking wistfully out to sea. He wished that it was in his power to give the great author what he wished for.

But that very night, Peter dreamed of a fabulous ship, with sails of silver and sheets of gold. It was the ship of dreams, and he ran on board as nimbly as he would have done when he was a boy. The places Peter visited that night and the people he met will remain a secret for ever, for his first and last great dream was one from which he did not awake. He has sailed on for ever, into the setting sun.

Princess
Dreamy

Once upon a time, there was a Princess who spent her life dreaming. Even in the middle of the day, you could find her sitting by herself, fast asleep or simply gazing into space. The King and Queen were rather worried about this, so they called all the most respected doctors in the land to give their considered opinions.

"It is a grave disease," said one doctor, "called *somnomulous revex*. Only very, very intelligent and sensitive people can catch it. Indeed, almost all the cases that have been recorded have been among royalty. Why, the King of Pandango suffered for years."

"And is there a cure?" asked the King, anxiously.

"Alas, Your Majesty, there are some afflictions that nobility must bear," said the first doctor. "I can prescribe some medicines that will ensure your daughter's good health, but I cannot take away her dreamy condition."

The second doctor stepped boldly forward.

"I must disagree with my learned colleague," he said. "The Princess's condition is not caused by an illness at all. She has clearly been bewitched. We shall need to find some powerful magic to counteract the spell that has been cast upon her. I could recommend someone, if Your Majesty wishes. I'm afraid that if an antidote to the spell is not found, your daughter will stay like this for ever."

"That's dreadful," said the King. "Yes, please, do give me the name of a reliable … er … spellbinder."

But the third doctor was already bustling forward.

"With all respect to my most esteemed colleagues," she said, "what I have heard so far has been complete nonsense from first to last. It is quite plain to me that someone has put a sleeping draught into your daughter's food. You should interrogate all your servants and have every morsel of her food checked by a reliable taster. I have the names of several reputable practitioners here if Your Majesty wishes. I can vouch for each and every one of them personally. I think Your Majesty will find that after a few days, the Princess will be her old self again."

"By all means give me the name of a good taster," said the King, although he privately wondered how his daughter was going to be able to eat *anything* if a taster ate every morsel – there wouldn't be any untasted morsels left!

Now a fourth doctor pushed his way to the front.

"We have heard a number of extraordinary opinions here today," he said, "and I don't doubt that my colleagues have all diagnosed your daughter in good faith, but they could not be more wrong. The Princess has quite obviously been hypnotised. It may have been a person who did it, or the Princess may have inadvertently hypnotised herself by listening too long to the ticking of a clock or the dripping of a tap."

"There are no dripping taps in *my* palace," put in the Queen, rather sharply. "But please do go on, doctor."

The fourth doctor blushed but continued.

"We shall need a very skilled treatment to bring the Princess back to her old self," he said. "Luckily, I myself trained in Zurich under the great Professor Pamplemouse. I would be willing to undertake the cure at once, but of course I would need all these people to be cleared from the room." With a sweeping gesture of his arm, the doctor indicated all the other doctors and courtiers standing around the King and Queen.

The King looked at his wife a little desperately. Then he turned to the crowd.

"Naturally, the Queen and I are anxious to do whatever is necessary to cure our only child," he said. "We have heard many learned opinions today, and we must think carefully about what to do. I beg you to leave us now and allow us to think over what you have said. We will give our decision in the morning."

The doctors bowed and walked backwards out of the room. Some of them were clearly not used to this manoeuvre, for they fell over their gowns and had to be rescued by the courtiers standing by. It was a sight that would normally have made the King roar with laughter, but today he was much too worried about his daughter to smile.

Soon there was no one in the room but the King, the Queen, the Princess and the little serving maid who looked after her. The Princess sat dreamily looking out of the castle window, paying no attention at all as the little maid combed her long, dark hair.

The King and Queen sat down together to discuss the opinions of the four doctors and decide what to do about their daughter.

"I don't know about *you*, my dear," said the King, "but I am well and truly confused. Can all these experts be right? Surely our darling girl cannot be so unfortunate as to be suffering from *somno*-something, *and* an evil spell, *and* a sleeping draught, *and* hypnotism all at the same time? That would be dreadful."

"I agree with you," said the Queen. "All of the diagnoses sounded sensible at the time, but now I don't know what to think. I suppose we could try each of the cures in turn?"

"And put our daughter through four lots of treatment?" asked the King. "That would surely make her worse than she is now. After all, it's not that she is in pain, or even unhappy. She just isn't exactly *with* us most of the time."

"You are right, my dear, of course," said the Queen. "Our daughter's wellbeing must be our first concern. But I am still uncertain about what to do."

Just then, a little voice from the corner of the room spoke up. It was the serving maid.

"Excuse me, Your Majesties," she said timidly, "but I spend a great deal of time with the

Princess. Might I just say something myself?"

"Of course you may," said the Queen kindly. "I know that you are very fond of your mistress and would not want any harm to come to her. What is your opinion of what we have heard today?"

"Well, Madam," said the little maid, curtseying deeply, "I have seven older sisters, and I have seen every one of them suffering from much the same illness as the Princess."

The King was a little shocked. "You mean it's not an illness that only royalty can suffer from?" he asked with a frown.

"I don't think so," said the little maid. "I think it is something that almost anyone can suffer from. My sisters were just like this. They sat by themselves. They sighed and didn't hear people talking to them. They gazed out of the window all the time. But I am very happy to say that each one of them has now recovered."

"So what was this illness from which they all suffered?" demanded the King, although the Queen was beginning to look as though she understood, and a small smile played about her lips.

Before the little maid could answer, she turned to the King and said, "You know, I had forgotten, but I believe I suffered from much the same malady around the time I first met you, my dear."

The maid smiled too, for the Queen was blushing and looking very pretty.

"Well, you two seem to know what you're talking about," muttered the King, a little gruffly. "Suppose you let a chap who's still in the dark into the secret?"

The little maid curtseyed again. "To put it plainly, Your Majesty," she said. "I believe that the Princess is in love."

"In love?" cried the King. "Why, that's preposterous! She's much too young, and besides, who can she possibly have met that she could be in love with?"

"Don't be so silly, dear. She is two years older than I was when I married you," said the Queen briskly. "And if you remember, young Prince Beaumont was here only last month. He stopped by on his way to visit his aunt, the Grand Duchess."

At the mention of Prince Beaumont's name, the silent Princess turned first white and then pink, causing the Queen and the serving maid to look triumphantly at each other. The King groaned loudly.

"I see only too clearly that I shall have no say in this matter," he said, "although in truth I like young Beaumont well enough, and it could have been much, much worse. If she wants that young Princeling, and he feels the same, I won't stand in their way."

At that, the Princess ran across the room and threw her arms around her father. Having spent several secret afternoons with the Prince, she knew only too well that he had the same feelings for her as she had for him.

The King was astonished, but pleased. And the Queen immediately began to plan the biggest royal wedding that the world had ever seen.

As for the little serving maid, she became a Lady-in-Waiting of the First Rank, for when it comes to knowing what is the matter with ordinary mortals, common sense is often a great deal more useful than any amount of learning, even from Professor Pamplemouse in Zurich!

The
House
That Slept

Now everyone knows that human beings are not the only creatures who like to curl up and go to sleep. Cats love to sleep in the sunshine. Ducks tuck their heads under their wings on the pond. And some animals, such as tortoises, sleep for months and months at a time. But did you know that houses sometimes sleep too? This is the story of a house that slept.

There was once a little house at the edge of a wood. It had red tiles on the roof and a green front door. It was a dear little house, and the family that lived in it loved it very much.

There were six of them altogether. Mr and Mrs Ruggles had four children. That was a lot of people to squeeze into a very little house, but they were a happy family and got along very well. Mr Ruggles worked in the woodland, clearing fallen branches and felling trees when the time was right. He walked to his work each day and enjoyed it enormously. He felt that he was a lucky man to live where he wanted to live and work where he wanted to work.

Mrs Ruggles worked in the nearby town. She was a nurse, visiting people in their homes and making sure that they were taking care of themselves properly. She too enjoyed her work. She even enjoyed the journey into town each day, driving along the pretty, winding road through the beautiful countryside.

The children went to school in the town too, but they were always glad to come home to their little house next to the wood.

The family took care of each other, and they took care of the little house, too. Each year, Mr Ruggles climbed up on to the roof (while Mrs Ruggles stood below and called to him to be careful) and checked that none of the red tiles were loose or broken. And every other year, Mr and Mrs Ruggles painted the front door and the windows, to keep out the rain and frost. As they grew older, the children helped with the painting, too, so that a job that once took a whole week was finished in two days.

The children grew up, as children do, and one by one they

left home to study, or work, or find homes of their own.

Soon, only Mr and Mrs Ruggles were left. At first the house seemed very big without the children, but Mrs Ruggles said that they couldn't possibly go and live somewhere smaller because the children would need somewhere to sleep when they came home for visits. Mr Ruggles was secretly very relieved to hear his wife say this. He loved living so near the forest, and he loved the old house. It had so many happy memories.

But time passed, and first Mr Ruggles and then Mrs Ruggles

retired from their work. They still loved their home, so they decided not to move, although their children all thought that would be a good idea.

"It's so lonely out here," they said. "What if one of you became ill and needed a doctor?"

Mr and Mrs Ruggles laughed.

"We're not quite in our dotage yet, you know!" they said.

But it was harder now to look after the little house, even without having to worry about work as well. Now that there were only the two of them to do the painting, it took three weeks – much longer than before. And they had to call a man out from the nearby town to check the tiles, because Mrs Ruggles said that it just wasn't safe for her husband to climb on to the roof any more.

There were other problems, too. Although he still liked to live near the wood and watch as it changed through the seasons, Mr Ruggles was upset by the way his old work was now done by machines and lads who had no feeling for the beautiful trees.

"It's not the same," he said. "It breaks my heart to see them carting logs away as if they were sacks of coal. Those trees are living things. They should be treated with respect."

Then, one very cold winter, snow lay so thickly around the little house that Mr and Mrs Ruggles were trapped for two weeks. They were no longer strong enough to clear the snow from the driveway, and they were worried about dangerous ice on the winding road into town.

The couple sat in their armchairs either side of the fire and looked at each other.

"We've had a wonderful time in this old house," said Mr Ruggles, "but it's time we moved into a little bungalow in town."

"Yes," said Mrs Ruggles. "I shall be sad to leave here, but it will be a relief, too, in a way."

So Mr and Mrs Ruggles locked the green front door for the last time and followed the van containing their furniture and all their possessions along the winding road. They were very happy in their new home and soon hardly ever thought of the little house near the wood.

Meanwhile, a board was put up outside the house. "To Let," it said. "Contact Buttle and Bung, Estate Agents." Several people came to look at the house, but it was either too small, or too far from town, or too lonely, or too old-fashioned. After a few months, the estate agents' board fell down in a high wind, and no one bothered to put it up again. Standing by itself, next to the lovely woodland, the house fell fast asleep.

Of course, it didn't shut its eyes, for houses don't have eyes, but they have windows, and these gradually grew dull and dusty. The paint on the front door began to fade and peel. The red tiles, which Mr Ruggles had looked after so carefully, began to slip and slide, and some of them fell off altogether.

Then, of course, the rain began to trickle into the house. It dripped through the ceilings and made puddles on the floors.

But the house wasn't empty. Oh no. All kinds of little creatures made their home there. Spiders filled the corners with cobwebs. Little ants and beetles crept along the dusty floorboards. Moths fluttered around the windows. In the walls, little feet could be heard scampering night and day, as a group of mice moved in and brought up their own families. An owl perched on the guttering some moonlit nights.

So the house slept on, and the trees crept nearer to it, until their branches touched the roof and pushed more of the tiles into the garden. Well, it wasn't a garden any more, really. The plants rampaged everywhere, and some of them reached right up to the bedroom windows. If you weren't looking carefully, you could walk right past the house and not know it was there. It was having a long, long sleep.

Then, one day, Mr and Mrs Ruggles' eldest son came back to visit the place where he had grown up. He brought his wife and their two young children with him.

"I'm so looking forward to seeing it," said the younger Mrs Ruggles. "You've talked so much about it. I'm sure it was a perfect place for a child to live."

When he turned off the long, winding road from town, her husband couldn't believe his eyes. The trees and hedges along the drive had grown so much.

"It all looks so different," he said. "And, oh no, I don't believe it! The house has gone!"

"No," said his wife, for she had seen a chimney sticking up above the bushes. "It's still here, hidden behind all this greenery."

"It's a secret house," laughed the children. "Let's go and look inside! It's an adventure!"

It took ages to push aside the branches and wade through the grass to the front door. The lock had rotted away, so it was easy to swing the door back on its creaking hinges and step inside.

"Be careful," warned Mr Ruggles. "The floorboards may

have rotted, and it doesn't look as if the ceiling is too safe either."

The grown-ups and the children tiptoed through the rooms. The house was in a terrible state, but somehow it still felt like a happy place to be.

As the children ran out to explore the garden – which they called "the jungle" – their mother and father looked at each other and saw that they were both thinking the same thing.

Mrs Ruggles laughed. "It would be mad!" she said. "There's so much work to do on it!"

Mr Ruggles smiled too. "It would be stupid," he agreed.

His wife sighed. "It would be a wonderful place for the children to grow up," she said.

"We'd never find another house in such a beautiful spot," said her husband.

Soon they were both giggling like children.

"It's time we did something completely crazy again," said Mr Ruggles. "Let's go and explore the jungle."

Over the next few weeks, there was more activity around the house than there had been for the last ten years. Trees were cut down, and bushes were pruned. Soon it was possible to reach the

front door without a struggle.
But still the house slept.

Over the next few months,
workmen hammered and sawed.
Timbers were renewed and
floorboards replaced. New red
tiles were put on the roof, and
the front door was mended and
painted – green, of course. But
still the house slept.

At last the day came when Mr
and Mrs Ruggles and their two
children moved in. Lights winked
at the windows, and the house
felt a warmth inside that had
been missing for a long time. The
house stretched and creaked for
a moment – and woke up at last.

Wake Up,
Muffin!

Cats look so comfortable when they are asleep. Somehow they always manage to find the warmest, cosiest spot in the whole house. And often it's the very spot where you most want to sit yourself!

But some cats seem to want to sleep most of the time, and that can be particularly annoying if what you'd really like to do is to play with them.

Helena had a cat called Muffin. The little girl loved him very much. She couldn't remember him when he was a kitten, because she was only a baby herself then, but even now,

Muffin wasn't an old cat. He was only four, just like Helena.

But Helena was a lively little girl, and Muffin was a very sleepy cat. Very often, when Helena wanted Muffin to join in one of her games, he was fast asleep on the sofa.

"Wake up, Muffin!" Helena would call, bending close to one of the cat's furry little ears.

Muffin's ear would twitch, just a little bit.

"Wake up, Muffin!" Helena would shout, louder this time, bending a little closer.

Muffiin's ear would twitch a little bit more.

Helena would take a deep
breath and lean forward until she
was almost touching the soundly
sleeping cat.

"Wake up, Muffin!" she would
yell, so loudly that her mother
could hear her from the kitchen.

And Muffin? He would open
one lazy eye. He would twitch
his whiskers and have a little
stretch. And he would go right
back to sleep again.

It was so annoying! Helena
tried being extra specially nice to
Muffin. She stroked his fur gently
and tickled his fat tummy. She
sang him little songs about mice
and kittens. But nothing worked.

Muffin would simply purr with pleasure and stay fast asleep.

One day, Helena badly wanted Muffin to play with her. She was tired of her dolls, who were nothing like as warm and cuddly as her cat. She put her doll in its pram and tucked a quilt round it.

"You just go to sleep like a good girl, Hettie-Marie," she said (for that was the doll's name).

Helena searched everywhere for Muffin. He wasn't on the sofa, which was his favourite place. He wasn't under the table or next to the radiator. At last she found him fast asleep (of course!) on the quilt of her parents' bed.

As she looked down at the sleeping cat, Helena had a brilliant idea.

She bent down and gently put her arms around Muffin. He wasn't very heavy as she lifted him up and cuddled him next to her, and he didn't move a muscle. He was fast asleep as usual.

Helena carried Muffin into her bedroom. She took silly Hettie-Marie out of her toy pram and tucked Muffin in instead. He looked so sweet!

All day, Helena played with her new baby. And what a good baby he was! He didn't cry and he didn't try to climb out of his bed.

He looked lovely wrapped up in a lacy shawl, and he looked absolutely gorgeous with a little blue bonnet on his head!

Best of all, when Helena lifted him out of his pram or his cradle and held him in her arms, he was warm and cuddly, not cold and hard like her dolls.

So now, if you visit Helena's house, you hardly ever hear a piercing shout of "Wake up, Muffin!" ringing through the place. In fact, you are much more likely to hear Helena complaining very quietly when her mother makes a noise with the vacuum cleaner or shuts a door rather more loudly than usual.

"Ssssh!" she will say, frowning fiercely. "Can't you do that a little more quietly, please? You'll wake Muffin!"

Goodnight,
Little Elf!

Once upon a time, there was a little elf who lived in a tree. It was a beautiful big house, with a smart door and four little windows at the front. The elf loved her home, but it was rather old. One day storm clouds gathered and a great wind swept through the forest. With a creaking and a crashing, the tree-trunk house tumbled to the ground. Luckily its branches cushioned the fall, and it fell with its windows pointing to the sky, so the little elf was not hurt and managed to climb out of her own front door. But her beloved home was lost for ever.

Now elves live in all kinds of places. You will find them in toadstools and among the roots of hedgerows. They may borrow an abandoned bird's nest or make a cosy house in a deserted rabbit's burrow. In fact, they can live almost anywhere. The only place that elves really don't like

to live is somewhere that has humans nearby. Elves are always a little bit afraid that humans will try to catch them and keep them captive. Perhaps they are right.

The little elf in this story, whose name was Periwinkle, set to work straight away to find a new place to live. She was very sad to leave her old home, but she really didn't have any choice. She was always a happy, practical little elf, so she made the best of the situation and began her search.

Unfortunately, it wasn't very easy. The storm had happened just as winter was passing into spring, and in springtime, as you know, little creatures are all finding or building homes to have their babies in.

It seemed to poor Periwinkle that every burrow she looked in had a mother rabbit already in residence. And every nest that she thought was abandoned had a bright-eyed little bird making essential repairs before the important egg-laying season.

What about toadstools? I hear you asking. Well, it was a strange thing, but there just didn't seem to *be* many that year. It's like that with living things. Some years there seem to be, say, ladybirds everywhere, and sometimes you can hardly find any.

The nights were still cold in early spring, so Periwinkle really needed somewhere cosy to spend the night. Luckily, she had lots of woodland friends who let her snuggle down on their floors for a night or two, but Periwinkle knew that they too would soon have houses full of little ones, and there would be no room for her. She really did need to find a home of her own.

Then, one afternoon, when Periwinkle was searching on the very edge of the wood, she came to a wire fence. It was the kind

that has great big holes in it, so
it was easy for the little elf to
climb through. The other side of
the fence looked very wild and
overgrown, so she didn't think
for a moment that it might be
part of a human garden.

Periwinkle made her way
through the long grass. There
were one or two old apple trees,
but they looked as though no
one was looking after them.
There were some brambles and
thistles, but they both looked
rather prickly for an elf's home.

Suddenly, Periwinkle saw a
little house in a tree! It wasn't as
nice as her old home at all, but it

made Periwinkle's eyes light up all the same. It would be lovely to live in a tree again!

The trunk was surprisingly easy to climb, so the little elf

quickly clambered up it and peeped into the little house.

It looked as though it hadn't been lived in for a very long time. There was no furniture and there were no curtains at the single window. In fact, the treehouse was completely empty.

Periwinkle could hardly contain her excitement. It wasn't ideal for an elf, being rather high and draughty, but it was in a tree and it was empty. She would move in straight away!

Over the next few weeks, Periwinkle made the treehouse as comfortable as she could. It wasn't possible to do much about the open door and window, although she did have a word with one or two friendly spiders and asked them to spin their webs across the openings to shut out the whistling wind just a little.

But Periwinkle soon made herself some furniture from acorns and twigs. Before a week had passed, she had a chair, a table and a little bed. The treehouse was beginning to feel like home!

As Periwinkle worked on her new house, spring passed. The weather became warmer and the nights grew lighter. Soon it didn't matter that the wind could blow through the window and door. It was pleasant to have a cool breeze on her face when the sun was at its hottest.

Periwinkle was now so happy in her new home that she never even thought about who had built it. So one summer's evening, she was very, very surprised to hear someone big and heavy climbing up the tree.

Bare as the treehouse was, there was nowhere for the little elf to hide. She stared in horror as the face of a big human boy appeared at the door. In seconds, his big human body followed. He

seemed to fill the whole
treehouse as he came clumping
across the floor. And then he
noticed Periwinkle.

"Hello!" he said.

Periwinkle wanted to run away,
but the boy was between her
and the door. She wanted to
hide, but there was nowhere to
go. Most of all, she wanted to
disappear into thin air, but
although elves are very clever at
a great many things, they can't
do magic like that.

So Periwinkle really didn't
have much choice but to talk to
the human. He seemed huge, but
she realised that he was

probably not very old at all, and he did *look* friendly.

"Hello," said Perwinkle in her turn. "How do you do?"

"I'm very well, thank you," said the boy politely. "Are you a fairy?"

"Goodness me, no!" said Periwinkle. "Fairies are quite different. I'm an elf. We don't have wings, you see, and we're much more sensible than fairies."

"Hmm, I always thought fairies were rather silly," said the boy. "It's interesting that you agree with me."

He looked around the tidy treehouse and saw Periwinkle's little chair, table and bed. He even noticed the cobwebs across the window. (I'm afraid he had broken the ones across the door when he came in.) For a human, he really was quite observant, thought Periwinkle.

"Have you been here long?" asked the boy.

"Since early spring," said the little elf. She was feeling much more comfortable now. He didn't look like the kind of boy who was going to put her in a jar and show her to all his friends. The next thing she knew, she was telling him all about her beloved treehouse and the great storm that had destroyed it.

"I remember that night," said the boy. "Our gates were blown right off their hinges."

There was a small silence. Then the boy said, "I'm Jake, by the way. Who are you?"

"Periwinkle," said the little elf. "I'm very pleased to meet you, although I've never spoken to a human before."

"If it comes to that," laughed the boy, "I've never spoken to an elf! This has been quite a day."

Well, the little elf and the boy talked for a long time, until they heard his mummy's voice calling from the other end of the garden.

"Jake! Jake! Where are you?"

At once, Periwinkle looked frightened out of her wits.

"What's the matter?" asked Jake. "It's only my mother. She's quite nice really."

Then Periwinkle explained about how elves are afraid of humans, and the boy looked as if he understood.

"There are things that I'm afraid of too," he said. "And you don't have to worry about me telling anyone about you. I think my friends would laugh, you know. I don't think boys are meant to see elves, any more than elves are meant to talk to boys. You can be a secret."

"And you can be a secret, too," said the little elf. "My elf friends wouldn't like it if they knew I talked to you either."

"Well, I must go now," said Jake. "But I'll come and see you again tomorrow, if that's all right."

"That will be *lovely*," said Periwinkle. "Goodnight, boy!"

"Goodnight, little elf!" laughed Jake. "Goodnight!"

The Day
the Sun
Was Silly

Most people are awake in the daytime and asleep at night. Well, that doesn't always work for babies! And there are people who have to work at night as well. But on the whole, we get up when the sun gets up and go to bed when the sun goes to bed.

Of course, the sun doesn't really go to bed. It just shines on another part of the world. It is always daytime *somewhere* in the world. And it is always night somewhere else, as well. It works very well. We all get a share of the sun for part of the day.

But long, long ago, there was a day when the sun was very silly.

All day long, he had been shining down on a beautiful garden. There were flowers and trees, grass and fountains. It was lovely. The flowers lifted their pretty faces to say hello to the sun, and the tiny drops of water that jumped from the fountains sparkled like little jewels in the sunlight. The sun had never seen a more perfect sight.

"What a shame it will be night time soon," said the sun, "and I will not be able to shine on this garden any more. It's all very annoying. After all, I'm much bigger than anything else in the sky. I should be able to decide what I can do. No one's powerful enough to argue with *me*!"

So the silly sun carried on shining on the beautiful garden. The flowers stayed open, and the birds carried on singing.

But the garden wasn't meant to have sunshine all the time. Soon the flowers began to droop in the hot sun. The birds began to get hoarse from singing for so long.

The sun was stubborn. He wanted to prove that he could do anything he liked. He was determined to carry on shining whatever happened.

Of course, the garden wasn't the only place that was in

trouble. All over the world people were feeling very confused.

Streetlights came on and looked quite out of place in the bright sunshine. Animals that like to come out at night, such as owls, didn't know what to do. They were hungry, but it was much too bright to fly out of their nests.

In other parts of the world, there was the opposite problem. It was still dark, long after it should have been daytime. Some people were still in bed, asleep. Others tried to carry on as usual, eating their breakfast in the dark and setting off for work or school with torches. It was quite hopeless. And all because the silly sun thought he could do whatever he liked.

Meanwhile, the moon was getting very cross. If the sun kept shining, *she* couldn't be seen at all. The stars were invisible too.

Across the huge distances of space, the moon called out to the silly old sun.

"Hey! What do you think you're doing? Everything is dreadful on earth because you're not doing as you should. We all look up to you, you know."

When he heard that, the sun felt ashamed. He looked down on the beautiful garden and saw that the flowers were drooping and the birds were dropping off their perches with tiredness.

"They all rely on me," he thought. "I must be a sensible old sun in future."

And you know, from that day to this, he has never been silly again. Thank goodness!

Bubbles
at
Bathtime

Once upon a time, there was a little boy who really hated his bathtime. He would yell and scream and kick his feet. It was terrible. And the funny thing is that there wasn't anything about his bath itself that he didn't like.

Here is what had happened. When Robert was a little tiny boy, he enjoyed being up and about so much that he never wanted to go to bed. He soon learned that bathtime meant bedtime would soon follow, so he started protesting as soon as his mummy began to run the water. It was dreadful. The yelling and screaming and kicking were so horrible that his poor mother dreaded bathtime more than cleaning the oven or opening the electricity bill.

The silly thing is that the yelling and screaming and kicking made Robert so tired that he always fell asleep the moment his mummy popped him into his little bed. So nobody realised that it was really bedtime and not bathtime he didn't like.

Sometimes we carry on doing things even when we can't remember why we do them any more. They become a habit. Bathtimes were like that for

Robert. Although he was quite a big boy now, nearly old enough to go to school, he still made a dreadful fuss at bathtime.

One morning, Robert received a surprise parcel. It wasn't his birthday or anything like that, so he couldn't wait to open it. Mummy looked at the writing and said she thought it was from Aunty Sue.

Robert liked Aunty Sue. She always sent him presents that were just right. He tore off the outer wrapping. Inside the brown paper was another parcel, wrapped in coloured paper. This one had a strange label:

My name is Bubbles

Whatever did *that* mean? As he ripped away the wrapping paper, Robert's face fell. Inside was a toy duck, the kind you have in the bath. It was quite a nice duck, certainly, with a yellow body and an orange beak, but still it was babyish, he thought. And anyway, it reminded him of that word beginning with *b*!

Robert pushed the duck across the table in disgust and hurried off to play.

That night, as Robert kicked and screamed in his bath, he noticed that his mother had put the duck on the shelf near the taps. Remembering his awful disappointment earlier in the day made Robert yell even more.

Just when Robert's poor mother was thinking that she couldn't stand *any* more, the telephone rang. There was a telephone out on the landing, so the poor woman quickly went to answer it, leaving the bathroom door open so that she could see her son all the time and make sure he was all right.

"Hello?" said Robert's mummy.

"Hello!" said Bubbles the duck.

What? Robert stopped his screaming for a moment in surprise. He thought for a moment that the duck had spoken, but of course that was silly.

"Hello," said Bubbles again. "It's Robert, isn't it?"

"Yes," said Robert, before he'd had time to think.

"Well, what's the trouble?" asked the duck in a friendly way.

"The trouble?" asked Robert, still not able to believe his ears.

"Yes. I couldn't help noticing, you see, that you were making quite a noise just now. Is something the matter?"

Robert shook his head like a puppy dog. He thought he might have water in his ears. There must be some reason why he kept thinking the duck was speaking. And here it was doing it again!

"Well?" the duck persisted. "Is something wrong?"

"No," said Robert. "Yes, no!"

"You don't seem to be able to make up your mind," commented Bubbles. "Is the bath too hot or cold for you?"

"No," said Robert, rubbing his eyes in disbelief.

"Are you afraid of water?"

"No," said the little boy again.

"Well, is it soap you don't like?"

"No, soap is all right," said Robert, frowning.

"I'm sorry," said the duck. "I simply don't understand. Why were you screaming and yelling if you don't mind having a bath?"

Robert looked down. He felt rather silly.

"I don't know," he said.

"You don't know? A big boy like you? Well, that is very strange. I must say that in all my years of being in baths, I've never seen anything like it."

"Haven't you?" asked Robert, feeling very small.

"Certainly not," said the duck firmly. "Now is this kind of thing going to continue? Because I'm not sure I can live next to a bath that has such a noisy boy in it."

Robert thought for a minute. "I don't think I'm going to do it any more," he said, to his surprise.

"Good," said Bubbles. "Then I'll be happy to stay."

Later that week, Robert heard his mother talking to a friend.

"You know," she said, "all these years of screaming and all he wanted was for me not to be in the room. After all, he's nearly old enough to go to school. Why ever didn't I think of it before?"

Well, I'm not going to tell her what really happened. Are you?

Mr Potter's Problem

It was two o'clock in the morning. As usual, Mr Potter was down in the kitchen, making himself a cup of tea. At two o'clock in the morning? Well, yes. You see Mr Potter simply couldn't sleep. Rather than lying awake, staring into the darkness, he felt it was better to come down and have a comforting cup of tea. At least from here he couldn't hear the dreadful noise.

You see, after thirty years of married life, Mr Potter's wife had started to snore. It wasn't just a gentle snuffling noise. It was an awful, trumpeting, elephant-on-the-warpath sort of noise. It was the kind of thing you couldn't sleep through no matter how hard you tried. And Mr Potter had tried very hard indeed.

The first thing he had tried was Mind over Matter. If I just pretend I can't hear it, he thought, I *won't* hear it, and I'll be able to get back to sleep.

Well, I don't know if you've ever *tried* to sleep through a deafening elephant-on-the-warpath trumpeting noise, but it's not very easy. Just as the echo of the snore is dying away, and you are drifting off to sleep again, an ear-splitting blast hits you amidships.

Mr Potter was a practical man, so the next thing he tried was Double Strength Ear Plugs. The label on the packet claimed that you could sleep through a hurricane with this wonderful product in place. Well, maybe you could, but you couldn't sleep through Mrs Potter's snoring, as Mr Potter can confirm. It was slightly softer, oh yes, and sort of muffled too, but in a way that was worse. With ear plugs in, Mr Potter felt as though the noise was inside his own head. It was really horrible.

Now you will be asking, why didn't Mr Potter do the sensible thing and hop off to spend the night in the spare room, where the snoring would sound like a faraway bugle call. Well, Mr Potter was a really kind man, and he was determined that his wife wouldn't find out about her problem from *him*. You see, Mrs Potter was a proud and proper woman. She wouldn't have dreamed of letting the next-door neighbours see her in her curlers or of wearing her slippers in the street. Her kind husband knew that she would be mortified if she knew about the snoring, so he was doing everything he could to keep the news from her, but, oh dear, the poor man was beginning to feel faint from lack of sleep!

Mr Potter went to the library to read up about the causes of snoring. Before long he had a whole pile of books open in front of him. It seemed that there were as many views about how to solve the problem as there were people who snored.

But one paragraph caught Mr Potter's eye. It claimed that a lack of fresh air could make matters worse.

That night, as they were getting ready for bed, Mr Potter said casually to his wife, "It's quite warm tonight, my dear. Do you mind if we have the window open a little? I read in the paper that it's terribly important to have plenty of fresh air when you get to our age."

"It's terribly important not to catch pneumonia too," said his wife, "but I suppose it *isn't* very cold tonight, so if you'd like the window open, that's fine."

Mr Potter smiled to himself as he opened the window wide. Maybe this would do the trick.

Fifteen minutes later, Mr Potter was off to make an early cup of tea. The noise seemed *worse*! He was so tired that he actually nodded off at the kitchen table … and woke up five hours later with a stiff neck, just in time to crawl back to bed for another couple of hours of elephants.

Next morning, Mr Potter took himself off to the park for a brisk walk to clear his head. While he was gone, there came a knock at the door. When Mrs Potter went to answer it, she found her next-door neighbour looking embarrassed on the doorstep.

"Excuse me, Mrs Potter," said Mrs Maybury. "I wonder if I could have a word? It's a rather delicate matter, so perhaps I could come inside?"

"By all means," said Mrs Potter, who certainly didn't want the world and his wife knowing her business.

When the two ladies were sitting comfortably in the living room, Mrs Maybury seemed to be having some difficulty in knowing where to begin.

"Are you feeling quite well?" asked Mrs Potter. "You look pale."

"The fact is," said Mrs Maybury, grateful for a place to start, "I haven't had a wink of sleep all night. That's why I've come."

Mrs Potter was puzzled. "I'm not sure how I can help," she said slowly.

"You see, the reason I can't sleep," confessed Mrs Maybury, "is your husband."

Mrs Potter almost fell out of her chair. For one wild moment she imagined that Mrs Maybury had taken a fancy to Mr Potter and was unable to sleep for thinking of him. Then she pulled herself together and realised she was being ridiculous. Mr Potter was a dear, sweet man, and the love of her life, but he was hardly the stuff that dreams are made of.

"I shall have to ask you to explain," said Mrs Potter rather stiffly to her neighbour.

"Oh, please don't be angry," cried Mrs Maybury, hearing Mrs Potter's tone. "I know it's embarrassing, but we have lived next door to each other for twelve years now. We should be able to talk about these things like mature human beings."

"But what things?" asked Mrs Potter, feeling as though she was wading through treacle.

"Why, Mr Potter's *snoring*," said Mrs Maybury.

Mrs Potter was more surprised than she would have been if Mrs Maybury *had* conceived a passion for Mr Potter.

"His snoring?" she gasped.

"Yes," moaned Mrs Maybury. "We hear it every night, you know. The walls are quite thick between our houses. I never hear your television or your vacuum cleaner or anything. But that snoring positively shakes the walls! We've been hearing it for some time, but it wasn't loud enough to disturb us, and I didn't like to say anything. Last night was the final straw. I think you had your window open, and we did too. It was deafening! I lay awake all night, and so did my husband."

"Indeed?" said Mrs Potter coldly. She didn't take kindly to criticism, and Mrs Maybury was beginning to annoy her. "I can truthfully say that it has never disturbed *me*," she went on, "but then I am a sound sleeper, not *foolishly nervous* or worried by *silly little things*. I do realise that not everyone has my excellent health and clear conscience."

"Well, I did feel I should mention it," said Mrs Maybury, rising to her feet.

"And I'm very glad you did so," said Mrs Potter warmly. "I do hope it has helped you to get it off your chest, my dear."

Mrs Potter showed her neighbour to the door, and Mrs Maybury, feeling oddly as though it was *she* who had the problem, hurried home to report to her husband that the meeting had not been an unqualified success.

As soon as she had closed the front door, Mrs Potter picked up the telephone and got to work. She knew perfectly well that her neighbour was a truthful woman, and she didn't doubt for a moment that what she had said

was true, although it certainly
was extraordinary that she
herself had never been woken by
Mr Potter's snoring. Mrs Potter
was taking no chances. She
didn't want any more neighbours
coming round to complain, and
she wasn't going to run the risk
of her own sleep being disturbed,
now that she knew about Mr
Potter's "Little Problem".

By the time her husband came
home from his walk, Mrs Potter
had made her plans and was
ready to put them into action.
She made Mr Potter a cup of tea
and asked him to sit down as she
had something serious to say.

"Now, Alfred," she said, "you know that I've never been one to beat about the bush. I like to call a spade a spade. The fact is that the neighbours have been complaining about your snoring, so I've had to *take steps*. I've ordered a double-glazing firm to start work tomorrow, and, as I really can't afford to lose my sleep, I wondered if you could stay in the spare room until your little problem is better. I do realise you can't help it, dear."

Mr Potter opened his mouth to protest. Then he realised that his problems were at an end.

"Of course, dear," he said.

The
Wide-Awake
Christmas

Usually, it's not too difficult to get to sleep, but sometimes, if you are feeling poorly, or worried about something, or very excited, then it can be the hardest thing in the world.

Every year on Christmas Eve, twins Tommy and Joe just could not get to sleep. All night long, they would running along the landing to their parents' room with one important question.

"Has he been yet?" they would ask eagerly.

They meant Father Christmas, of course.

Daddy would groan and turn over. Mummy would call out.

"Go back to bed, Tommy and Joe. You'll be so tired in the morning, you won't be able to stay awake to open your presents *if* Father Christmas brings you any. I don't know what he'll have to say about two such naughty little boys."

"Oh, don't tell him! Don't tell him! We'll be good!" cried Tommy and Joe.

"We don't have to tell him," growled Daddy. "He knows *everything*. You just watch out."

And the twins would scamper back to bed and try ever so hard to shut their eyes and fall asleep. But it was *so* difficult.

Twenty minutes later, there would be little feet skipping across the landing again and right into Mummy's and Daddy's big bedroom.

"Has he been yet?" the little boys would whisper, tugging at the quilt.

"He *did* come," their father would whisper back, "but he heard that two bad little boys were not asleep, so he went away again. He *may* come back, but only if you shut your eyes and *keep* them shut."

As fast as their little legs would carry them, the boys would hurry back to their beds. But did they go straight to sleep until morning? Oh no. Ten minutes later they were off again. This time the question was different.

"Is it morning yet?" asked Joe.

Daddy muttered and mumbled and sat right up in bed.

"Do *you* think it's morning?" he said, looking at the bedside light. Its hands were glowing in the dark. They said half past three.

"It might be," said Tommy, hopefully. "Then we can open our presents.

"It's *dark*," moaned Daddy. "It's the middle of the night. It's ages and ages and ages until morning. *Go* back to bed and don't come back until you can see that it's getting light outside. Do you understand, both of you?"

Tommy and Joe nodded their heads and went back to their room. But did they snuggle back into bed? Oh no. They stood on tiptoes so that they could see out of the window. They wanted to be ready the very *moment* it began to get light.

It was a pity that a tree blowing in the wind made the next-door neighbour's outside light come on only fifteen minutes later.

Mummy and Daddy were drifting back to sleep when ...

woomph! ... *woomph!* ... two little bodies jumped right in the middle of their tummies.

"It's morning. It is! It is!" shouted the boys, bouncing up and down.

I'm afraid that what Daddy said then is really not repeatable. Luckily it was muffled by the quilt. Five seconds later, two little boys were being dragged unceremoniously across the landing and plonked ...*one!* ... *two!* ... in their beds.

"If I hear a peep out of either of you in the next three hours, I won't answer for my actions," yawned Daddy, pulling the curtains firmly shut and making the fiercest face he could.

What do you think happened? I won't go into the details, but by half past four, Mummy and Daddy had given up and were hugging cups of coffee in the sitting room, while two excited little boys opened a wonderful pile of presents.

Sometimes, you just have to give in gracefully.

When it was nearly time for the next Christmas, however, Daddy put his foot down.

"Now, I want a word with you boys," he said. "You know we have Granny coming to stay this Christmas. She's an old lady, and she won't want to be woken up in the middle of the night. You could make her very ill. You are both big boys now, so I want you to promise me that you won't come out of your room until it is morning. You've got your own big teddy bear clock now. When the little hand is pointing straight down and the big hand is pointing straight up, you can get up. That's still very early, but it isn't the middle of the night. Now, is it a deal?"

"Yes, Daddy," said Joe.

"Yes, Daddy," said Tommy.

The boys loved their granny. They certainly wouldn't want to do anything to upset her.

To the twins' parents, it seemed as if Christmas Eve arrived far too quickly. To the boys, the days seemed to crawl past. But at last it was here, and daddy went to collect Granny from the station.

"Happy Christmas, boys!" she called, as she came through the front door. Tommy and Joe couldn't help noticing that she had two bulging bags of presents and a suitcase that looked as if it was about to burst.

That evening, the whole family had a special Christmas Eve supper, with crackers and candles. The boys were almost unbearably excited.

"Now, it's bedtime for you two," said Mummy at last.

"Goodnight, boys," smiled Daddy. "Now, remember what I said, won't you?"

"Goodnight, darlings," said Granny. And, much to their surprise, she winked at them, careful that Daddy shouldn't see.

Tommy and Joe went to their bedroom and put on their pyjamas. They climbed into their beds and turned off the light.

A few moments passed.

"Are you asleep?" whispered Tommy to his twin.

"No," whispered Joe, "are you?"

The boys lay staring into the darkness. They could just see the luminous hands of their teddy bear clock. It was *hours* until the hands would be pointing straight up and straight down.

Time passed *so* slowly. It almost seemed as though the hands of the clock were going backwards! There was no way that the boys could get to sleep.

"This is going to be a *long* night," groaned Joe.

Later still, the twins heard their parents saying goodnight to Granny on the landing. The little strip of light at the bottom of the door disappeared as the landing light was turned off. Then there was silence.

More long, long minutes passed. The house was very, very quiet. Then the boys heard a funny little rustling sound and a tiny squeak as someone turned the handle of their door.

"Are you awake, boys?" said Granny's voice quietly.

"No!' whispered the twins.

"Good!" said Granny, coming into the room. "I don't know about you, but I never can get to sleep on Christmas Eve. It's much too exciting. I thought perhaps we could open one or two little presents to make the time pass more quickly. But you've got to promise to be very, very quiet. We don't want to wake up you-know-who, *do* we?"

Well, Granny and the twins had a wonderful time. Some of the presents were games to play, and it was even more fun playing and trying to be as quiet as mice at the same time.

Granny had sensibly brought one or two little Christmas snacks as well.

"Just to keep us going," she giggled, opening a tin of sausage rolls and cheese straws.

Unfortunately, they were all three having such a good time,

they didn't keep an eye on the clock. It was still dark when the big hand finally pointed straight up and the little hand pointed straight down.

Granny and the boys didn't notice the door silently opening.

"Mother!" cried Daddy. "You really are the limit!" But he was laughing until tears streamed down his face.

"You know the worst thing?" said Daddy later, when they were all downstairs. "Granny would never have let *me* open my presents early, when I was little!"

"Well," smiled his mother, "that's why *grannies* have more fun."

The
Bedtime
Bunny

Caroline's mother shook her head firmly.

"No," she said. "Not under any circumstances. Not tonight. Not tomorrow night. Not any night. Do you understand?"

Caroline opened her mouth to protest, but her mother had her I-will-not-change-my-mind-whatever-you-say face on, so she went meekly off to bed. It just wasn't fair.

The trouble was all about Caroline's fluffy white rabbit, Snowdrop. She wanted to take him to bed with her, but Mummy said it was out of the question. Poor Caroline, you are probably thinking. Why shouldn't she have her toy rabbit it bed with her? But Snowdrop wasn't a toy rabbit. He was real!

"Rabbits are cuddly and friendly, I know," Caroline's mother had said, "but, darling, they're not indoor animals. They belong outside. Snowdrop might make a terrible mess in your bedroom, and he really wouldn't be happy, you know."

Caroline was quite, quite sure her mother was wrong. Darling Snowdrop was always so pleased to see her when she went out to his hutch with a few green cabbage leaves.

He liked to play, too, when she
let him out of his hutch for a hop
around the garden. She had to be
very careful that he didn't hop
right away, but that wasn't
because he didn't like her, that
was because he was a very
adventurous bunny.

Caroline sat in her bedroom
and felt close to tears. It was a
cold night, and she felt sure that
Snowdrop would much rather be
with her in her warm little bed.
So do you know what that
naughty little girl did? She waited
until she could hear that her
mother was watching television
downstairs, then she put on her

slippers and dressing gown and crept out of the back door, taking her little torch with her.

Snowdrop seemed rather surprised to see her. Although the wind was whistling around his cage, he looked quite cosy and comfortable curled up in his pile of straw. In fact, when Caroline put her hands in to pick him up, he didn't really seem to want to come.

"You'll like it, Snowdrop, really you will," said the little girl. "But you mustn't make a noise as we go upstairs. All right?"

Caroline and her rabbit slipped through the back door and shut it carefully behind them. The little girl crept up the stairs as quietly as she could, which was quite difficult because Snowdrop would keep struggling. At last they were safely in Caroline's bedroom, with the door shut behind them.

Clutching her rabbit tightly, the little girl snuggled down in bed and stretched out her hand to turn off the light.

It should have been lovely, drifting off to sleep with her cuddly bunny in her arms, but, oh dear, Snowdrop was the *wriggliest* rabbit you have ever come across. And he was quite strong too. He wriggled and he jiggled and in the end he kicked Caroline so hard with his big back feet that she said, "Oh!" and let go of him.

With a *thump!* Snowdrop landed on the floor. Caroline heard him hopping off towards her toy cupboard before she had a chance to turn on the light.

Quickly, the little girl jumped out of bed and ran across the room to catch her rabbit.

"Come here, Snowdrop!" she called, as loudly as she dared. But Snowdrop was already knocking toys over and crashing around in the cupboard. Then he started to nibble the straw-stuffed paws of the little girl's favourite teddy bear!

Just then Mummy, who had been on her way upstairs and thought she heard a strange noise, popped her head round the door.

"Why is your light still on?" she asked. "Come on, darling. You've got school tomorrow."

Caroline swung round guiltily. She must make sure that her mother didn't see Snowdrop.

"I'm just getting into bed again, Mum," she said. "I just couldn't sleep because ... because ... because the wind was so loud."

Mummy looked at Caroline more suspiciously than she had done before.

"No, it isn't," she said. "What's going on in here?"

"Nothing," said Caroline, but she couldn't help taking a quick look towards the cupboard.

Caroline's mother didn't need any more clues. She strode over to the cupboard and flung the doors wide open.

There was nothing to be seen. Mummy peered here and there, but she couldn't see anything strange. Caroline held her breath. Snowdrop was being so good and quiet.

Then Mummy frowned and wrinkled up her nose.

"What's that *smell*?" she asked. "Something in this cupboard smells extraordinarily like a ... fluffy ... white ... *rabbit*!"

Just at that moment, Snowdrop hopped right out of the cupboard, leaving the smell, a half-chewed teddy bear, a scratched toy train and a squashed puppet behind him.

At first Mummy was really cross. Then she calmed down a little and said that she supposed there were some things that everyone just had to find out for themselves.

"Do you think Snowdrop was happy in your bed?" she asked.

"No," said Caroline.

"Do you think he was happy in your toy cupboard?"

"Well," said Caroline, "I think he did have quite a good time, yes, I do."

"And are *you* happy that he was in your toy cupboard?"

Caroline looked at the chewed teddy bear and damaged toys.

"No, not really," she whispered.

"Are you happy that you're going to have to clean everything in your cupboard and find out where that smell is coming from?" asked Mummy.

Caroline wrinkled her nose. "No, I'm not," she said.

"Are you happy that you didn't do what I said and told me stories when I came to see what was happening?"

"No." Caroline hung her head.

Mummy smiled and kissed her little girl.

"One more question, honey," she said.

"Where do you think rabbits really like to sleep?"

Caroline smiled. "In their hutches," she said, "outside."

I think she's right. Don't you?

The Dream Merchant

Once upon a time, there was a little boy who had the most wonderful dreams. His name was David. Every night when he closed his eyes, it was as though he walked into a wonderful new world. But David's dreams didn't just come to him by chance. He bought them from the dream merchant, who visited him as soon as his eyes were closed. And the dream merchant had his price, as you will see.

It happened like this. One day, David had been rather lazy at school. He didn't pay attention during his lessons, and the teacher spoke to him sharply.

"Do you have nice dreams at night, David?" she enquired, in front of the whole class.

"Sometimes," said David, looking puzzled.

"Then I'm surprised you need to dream during the day as well," said the teacher. "Perhaps your night-time dreams aren't exciting enough. I shall have to send the dream merchant to you."

Of course, all the children wanted to know what she meant, but the teacher just smiled mysteriously and would say nothing more.

That night, David went to bed as usual and fell asleep so

quickly that he didn't even have
time to turn his bedside lamp off.

"Good evening," said a magical
voice in his ear.

David felt as though he was awake, although he knew he was really asleep.

"Good evening," he replied.

"I'm the dream merchant," said the voice. "A friend of mine told me that you might like a visit. What kind of dream would you like to have?"

"Isn't this already a dream?" asked David.

"Oh," said the dream merchant, "everything is a dream in a way. It depends how you look at it. Have you thought yet? What would you like to dream about tonight?"

"Could I dream about pirates?" asked David, who had been

reading a very exciting book on just that subject.

"Of course," said the dream merchant. "Would you like an exciting dream, a scary dream, a comfortable dream, or a dream full of wonders?"

David wasn't sure. "I'd like an exciting dream," he said, "but could I have some … um … wonders as well?"

"No, no, only one kind at a time. You can have wonders tomorrow night if you like. An exciting dream it is. Now, what would you like to pay?"

"Pay?" echoed David. "What do you mean?"

"Well, I'm a merchant," said the magical voice a little impatiently. "I don't *give* things away, you know. I need something from you in return."

"What kind of something?" asked David.

"A whole day of paying attention at school, or a whole week of doing what your mother says, or a whole month of making your bed properly. Which shall it be?"

David didn't hesitate. "I'll pay attention at school tomorrow," he said.

With that, David heard a *woosh!* and a *whizz!* and he

found himself on the deck of a pirate ship.

When David woke the next morning, he found that his lamp was still on, with his pirate book lying beside it. His head was spinning from the amazing adventures he had had during the night.

That day at school, he started work on his pirate project, and the teacher was delighted with the way he concentrated and had such imaginative ideas.

"It's exciting, isn't it?" she said, but whether she meant the project or the visit of the dream merchant, David wasn't sure.

After that, the dream merchant came every night. In exchange for marvelous dreams, David helped his father in the garden and stopped teasing his little sister. He continued to pay attention at school. He was surprised to find that everything seemed to work a hundred times better when he just tried a tiny bit harder.

And so it was that a night came when the dream merchant visited as usual.

David asked for a dream about castles, and the dream merchant was happy to oblige. But when it came to thinking of a suitable payment, there was a problem. Everything the dream merchant suggested was something that David did already.

"You know," said David. "I've learnt that doing my best at things makes me happier all the time. I do it anyway, even if I don't have a dream to pay for."

"Then I think my work is done," said the dream merchant, with a smile in his voice. "From now on, you can make your own dreams. In fact, most of the time you can do anything at all that you want to do. You just have to try, that's all."

You could try it too. It's true!